SWAT
Secret World Adventure Team

Taste of
Thailand

by
Lisa Thompson

illustrated by
Brenda Cantell

PICTURE WINDOW BOOKS
Minneapolis, Minnesota

MISSION 800

ขอบคุณมาก

Editor: Jill Kalz
Page Production: Tracy Kaehler
Creative Director: Keith Griffin
Editorial Director: Carol Jones

First American edition published in 2006 by
Picture Window Books
5115 Excelsior Boulevard
Suite 232
Minneapolis, MN 55416
877-845-8392
www.picturewindowbooks.com

First published in Australia by
Blake Education Pty Ltd
CAN 074 266 023
Locked Bag 2022
Glebe NSW 2037
Ph: (02) 9518 4222; Fax: (02) 9518 4333
Email: mail@blake.com.au
www.askblake.com.au
© Blake Publishing Pty Ltd Australia 2005

Printed in the United States of America.

Library of Congress Cataloging-in-Publication Data
Thompson, Lisa, 1969-
Taste of Thailand / by Lisa Thompson ; illustrated by
Brenda Cantell.
p. cm. — (Read-it! chapter books. SWAT)
Summary: Ben and Lulu are recruited by the Secret World
Adventure Team for a mission in Bangkok, Thailand, where
they help a cook prepare special treats for the queen's
party at the Grand Palace.
ISBN 1-4048-1677-1 (hardcover)
[1. Adventure and adventurers—Fiction. 2. Cookery, Thai—
Fiction. 3. Bangkok (Thailand)—Fiction. 4. Thailand—Fiction.]
I. Cantell, Brenda, ill. II. Title. III. Series.
PZ7.T371634Tas 2005
[E]—dc22   2005027173

Every effort has been made to contact copyright holders of any material
reproduced in this book. Any omissions will be rectified in subsequent
printings if notice is given to the publishers.

Table of Contents

MYANMAR

LAOS

VIETNAM

THAILAND

BANGKOK

CAMBODIA

Gulf of Thailand

N

Kilometers
Miles
300

MALAYSIA

- POPULATION
  50 million
- OFFICIAL LANGUAGE
  Thai
- CURRENCY - Baht
- MAIN INDUSTRIES
  Tourism, Tin Mining, Rubber

CHAPTER 1
THE MISSION

Ben dangled the long, wriggling worm above his open mouth.

"You're not really going to swallow it are you? It's not even dead yet!" shrieked Lulu.

Ben let go of the worm, and it slipped down his throat.

"Yuck! You're so gross!" Lulu cried.

"It tasted OK. Your turn," said Ben.

"Forget it! I'm not playing anymore. I quit. You win. The game is all yours." Lulu walked away.

"Come on, Lulu. Don't be like that."
Ben walked to the back door. "Hey,
come and check this out."

"Forget it. I'm not falling for one of
your tricks. Game's over," Lulu said.

"Yeah, I heard you. But check this out.
It's a package for us," said Ben.

Lulu walked over. "So it is," she said. "This isn't one of your stupid jokes is it? Some weird, slimy thing isn't going to fall out when I open it?"

"I haven't seen this package before in my life. Honest. Here, just to prove it, I'll open it myself," Ben said, ripping the package open. Out fell a beeping black box flashing "PLAY ME."

A voice started:

"Hello, Ben and Lulu. Welcome to SWAT. And congratulations! Let me introduce myself. I am the voice of SWAT. My name is Gosic.

"SWAT is a top secret team whose name stands for Secret World Adventure Team. We have a database of every child in the world. We use it to find secret agents. We urgently need your help in Bangkok, Thailand, now!

hello Ben and Lulu...

"Your mission is to help chef Meh Dang prepare a feast for the queen's party at the Grand Palace tonight. You must leave at once! Do not delay.

"Inside this package you will find two transporter wristbands. You must wear them at all times. They will allow you to travel in the blink of an eye, and they will keep us in contact.

"Press **START MISSION** on the wristband to begin.

"Good luck, SWAT."

Ben and Lulu put on the wristbands.

"Are you sure this isn't one of your tricks, Ben?" asked Lulu, taking a good look at the wristband.

"I'm telling you, Lulu, I don't know what's going on," Ben said.

"Well, there's only one way to find out," she replied. "Ready? Three. Two. One."

Click.

START MISSION.

CHAPTER 2
LIN LEADS THE WAY

Plop! Plop! Plop, plop, plop! Huge raindrops fell on Ben and Lulu.

"Quick, let's take cover. It's pouring," said Lulu, pulling Ben through the rain.

They took shelter under a carved, golden doorway. Water rose up around their feet as the street gutters overflowed.

The door behind them opened, and a Thai girl with beautiful eyes and a big smile waved them inside. She bowed her head low and raised her hands to her forehead.

Lulu bowed and said, "Hello." When she looked up, the Thai girl was gone.

Lulu and Ben walked through the door
and into a courtyard. It was a wild
jungle of orchids, jasmine, and lush,
green plants. A narrow, winding path
led up to a doorway full of people.

"What do you suppose they're looking
at?" asked Ben.

"Let's find out," said Lulu, already halfway up the path. She peered over the crowd. "It looks like dancing," she whispered.

Women in bright, gold-trimmed silk swayed and jumped, their hands twisting and turning.

Suddenly, a masked dancer entered
and took over the stage. He danced in
a wild, uncontrolled way.

"He's the bad guy," said Ben with a grin.

The girl who had let them in turned and
smiled. "He is the dragon," she said.

The dragon dancer moved faster and faster. The music got louder and louder. TWANG! TWANG! TWANG! The dragon leaped through the air, a blur of silk tassels, his big mask shaking on his head. Then suddenly, he fell to the ground. The crowd clapped and shouted.

The Thai girl turned to Ben and Lulu. "The dancers are practicing for the queen's party tonight," she giggled. "My name is Lin. I am dancing at the party tonight, too."

"Hi, Lin. We need to find Meh Dang. Do you know where we can find her?" asked Ben.

"Ah. Meh Dang is very busy. She is cooking. Tonight, Meh Dang is going to serve her specialty, *goong den*, to the queen," Lin explained.

"What's goong den?" asked Lulu.

Lin smiled. "Tiny live shrimp get tossed into a bowl with hot spices. The spices make the shrimp go crazy. They leap and fly around. It can be funny trying to get them on your spoon. If you eat them fast enough, you can feel them wriggling down your throat."

"Sounds ... interesting," said Lulu.

Ben thought it sounded delicious. "I'd love to try that!"

"Follow me. I will show you where you can find Meh Dang," Lin said.

CHAPTER 3
BANGKOK STREETS

They ran out onto the busy Bangkok streets again. It was still raining, and Ben's shoes sloshed in the water as he tried to keep up.

"This is monsoon weather," Lin shouted through the rain. "When it rains heavily like this, the streets flood all the time."

She continued, "Bangkok is slowly sinking. It is because we built over the *klongs*. Klongs are the waterways that once ran through the city. Now there are only a few. But don't worry. We will not sink today. Today we will just get very, very wet!"

"Oh," said Lulu, splashing through the water. "That's a relief!"

The flooded streets had not stopped the traffic. Lines of cars and bikes snaked through the water, honking their horns. The noise was so loud that Ben and Lulu could hardly hear what Lin was saying.

They passed little shops and street vendors selling all kinds of things: watches, T-shirts, toys, bags, shoes, and food. Everyone had a smile—and a good price.

"You want to buy?" yelled a vendor. "Pick one, and I'll give you a good price."

Lin quickly bought some fish cakes and *satay* sticks from the food stand. Ben was relieved. All he had eaten that day was the worm.

In another shop, a crowd of people huddled around a television. They were watching Thai boxing.

"A very popular sport," said Lin. "Many people also play *takraw*. Do you?"

"What's takraw?" asked Ben, hardly taking his eyes off the action.

28

Lin pointed to a group of people standing in a circle playing with a small ball.

"You must keep the ball in the air using any part of your body, except your hands. The one who gets the ball through the hoop in the middle of the circle the most times is the winner. Maybe you will win!" Lin pointed to Ben and giggled.

Lin spoke to the group, and Lulu and Ben joined the circle. It was much harder than it looked. Ben had them all laughing as he used his face and head to score points.

Finally, Lin said, "We must go, or we will run out of time. I have to go to the *wat* this afternoon."

Lin saw by the look on their faces that they did not understand. She pointed to the closest temple, and they walked through the gate.

"A wat is a Buddhist temple. Most Thais are Buddhist. It is a very important part of our culture," Lin said.

A group of monks, wrapped in saffron-colored robes, walked past them. The monks were carrying bowls for people to place food in.

Families were making offerings of food, flowers, and incense. Lulu noticed many beautifully carved little buildings.

"What are they?" asked Lulu.

"They are spirit houses," Lin whispered. "Every house and building has a spirit house. We give offerings to the spirits inside so they will protect us."

They left the wat and finally arrived at a large, golden doorway.

"You will find Meh Dang in here," said Lin. "I must go now. I have many things to do. Maybe I will see you later when the rain stops." She laughed and disappeared into the crowded street.

33

CHAPTER 4
MEH DANG

Meh Dang was very upset. She was in the kitchen, and her voice was getting louder and louder. She was speaking very, very fast.

"I think she's about to burst," whispered Ben.

"I can't believe you used my jar of secret spices. I need it for tonight's goong den! Get out of my kitchen, and don't come back!" shouted Meh.

Pots, pans, woks, and bamboo steamers were flying everywhere. All of the kitchen helpers ran for cover. Meh stormed after them, still shouting.

Ben and Lulu crept slowly into the kitchen. They were overwhelmed with smells of all kinds. Jasmine and fresh coriander blended with basil and ginger. Each wonderful sauce smelled different: sweet, sour, salty, or spicy.

Ben couldn't resist, and he tasted one. It was orangey-red in color, smelled delicious, and dripped off his finger. He put his finger in his mouth, and the taste exploded on his tongue.

"AHHHHHHHHHHH. Hot! Hot! Hot!" he cried, as he grabbed a drink to stop the fire in his mouth.

"Let me guess, chili?" laughed Lulu.

"That was fast," Meh Dang said as she walked back in. "I sent for new kitchen helpers just two seconds ago. OK, let's get to work. We must go to the market and get the best and freshest ingredients. I must make a new batch of my special spices."

Meh Dang turned and left the kitchen. Ben and Lulu had to run to keep up with her.

The market was hot and crowded.
Everyone was talking fast and loud.
Meh haggled for a good price and
paid in baht, Thai money. She bought
herbs, spices, fruit, and vegetables.
Lulu and Ben had never heard of some
of the fruit before, such as rambutans,
mangosteens, and pomelos.

Ben held up a large, spiky fruit.
"What's this?" he asked.

"That is a durian. It's very good. You must try," said Meh.

It didn't smell too good, but if you held your nose, durian tasted delicious!

"Now we go to the klongs," said Meh.

She led them along crowded streets jammed with motorcycles and three-wheeled taxis. They passed dusty shops with birds in cages, people wanting to tell your fortune, and a shop that sold nothing but Buddha statues.

40

Then the trio reached the water.
They stepped aboard a longboat.
It twisted and turned down one
klong after another. They passed
other longboats filled with fruits
and vegetables.

Ben saw a boat piled high with sticky, fried bananas.

"That boat! Meh, take us to that boat!" cried Ben.

"You want some fried banana, Ben?" asked Meh with a smile. "I am very fond of fried banana myself."

They stopped by the boat and bought three sticky, fried bananas. They were soon giggling and licking their fingers.

Rickety, wooden houses on stilts lined the canals and were linked to each other by walkways even more rickety. As Ben, Lulu, and Meh motored along, they saw women washing clothes in the klong and children swimming. When their boat arrived at a house, a small group of people rushed out to meet them.

"Do you live here, Meh?" asked Lulu.

"No. I live in an apartment in the city. This is my family," she explained.

CHAPTER 5
MEH DANG'S FAMILY

Little faces peeked through the windows. Everyone was happy to see Lulu and Ben.

Meh's mother had prepared a meal, and she laid it all on mats on the floor. Everyone sat down on cushions and began to eat.

"You like the food?" asked Meh.

Lulu and Ben nodded, their mouths too full to reply.

"My dear mother is quite a wonderful cook. She taught me all I know," said Meh proudly.

One of the nephews wanted to give Lulu a present. His hands were cupped one over the other. Lulu held out her hand, and the boy dropped something into her palm.

"AAAAAAAAHHHHHHHHH," Lulu screamed, dropping the black, crawling surprise onto the ground. Everybody laughed. "What on Earth is it?" she asked, too afraid to look.

The shiny black bug lay on the floor as big as an egg, with a huge, pointed horn on its head.

"Rhinoceros beetle," laughed Meh. "Have you never seen one before?"

Lulu and Ben shook their heads.

Meh put the beetle on a piece of fruit.
"They are harmless. They eat only
plants and fruit. Their big horn is just
to scare you."

"Well, it worked!" laughed Lulu.

Later, Meh and her mother went into the kitchen to make another batch of special spices. Ben sniffed the spice bottle and almost passed out.

"Are you sure you want to use these, Meh?" Ben asked.

"You must use just the right amount, at just the right time, in just the right way. You wait and see. You will never have tasted such food," she said. "Now, my friends, it is time to go to the Grand Palace."

CHAPTER 6
MEH'S KITCHEN

The Grand Palace was more than grand. It was by far the most amazing building Ben and Lulu had ever seen. Gold leaf and mirror tiles lined the walls, making incredible patterns. Sculptures of Buddhist gods stood in the gardens and at the entrances.

"Why are the roofs shaped like that?" asked Ben on their way to the kitchen. The pointy roofs had spiky shapes at every corner.

"To keep bad spirits off the building," explained Meh.

They reached the kitchen, and Meh laid out the groceries. She checked through the ingredients, and a look of horror came over her face.

"Oh my goodness! The shrimp! How could I have forgotten?" She looked at the clock on the wall. "There is no time to go back and get them and prepare the rest of the dinner." Tears welled in her eyes. "What am I to do? How can I make goong den without shrimp? It's impossible!"

Lulu whispered to Ben, "I'll stay here and help Meh. You can use your SWAT wristband to go back to the market."

Ben nodded. "It's OK, Meh. I'll get the shrimp and be back before you know it." He walked behind a pillar and counted down. "Three. Two. One."

Click.

Meh and Lulu started chopping, slicing, dicing, and peeling. Meh showed Lulu how to wrap an egg roll.

Lulu wasn't very proud of her effort. It didn't look anything like the delicate roll Meh had made.

"Don't worry, Lulu.
It takes practice,"
Meh said.

They roasted cashews and peanuts for salads and dressings. Fish, soy and sesame sauce, shrimp paste, and lime juice all splashed around the wok.

Thick, rich, coconut cream cooled spicy dishes. There were red curries, green curries, yellow curries, and steamed curries. Noodles and rice flew in and out of the many pots.

Then they heard people starting to arrive for dinner. Hundreds of spring rolls and egg rolls were placed on trays, and waiters raced out with them. Plates went out full and came back empty. Lulu and Meh had red, shiny faces from the heat.

A waiter came through the door. "Meh, the queen is asking why you are keeping her waiting for the goong den. She doesn't want to eat too much before her favorite dish."

60

Meh's face was tense with worry. "What shall I do, Lulu? Should I tell them there is no goong den because I forgot the shrimp? I will look like a complete fool."

"It's OK, Meh. Ben will be back any minute. I'm sure of it," Lulu said.

Where was he? Lulu hoped he hadn't gotten lost.

At that moment, Ben walked into the kitchen holding a huge, watery bag full of live shrimp. He was puffing and panting and smelled very fishy.

Meh looked relieved. She yelled, "Quickly, Ben! Quickly! Bring the shrimp over here."

Meh took her special spices off the stove and put them into a bowl. Lulu poured some shrimp into a beautiful silver and gold serving bowl. A gong sounded in the dining hall as Meh left to serve her goong den to the queen.

CHAPTER 7
FIT FOR THE QUEEN

Meh placed the bowl in front of the queen and poured in her secret spices. The shrimp went crazy, leaping and twirling all over the place.

The queen laughed as she tried to catch them with a spoon. Her face lit up when she ate her first spoonful of Meh's goong den.

"She loved it, Meh!" cried Lulu. "Did you see her face? She looked like she had never tasted anything so good."

Meh nodded and smiled. "Would you like to try?"

"Yes, please!" said Ben.

"And Lulu? Go on, have a try. You may be pleasantly surprised," Meh said, handing them each a bowl of wriggling shrimp.

Ben caught one and placed it in his mouth. It wriggled right down his throat. It tasted amazing. He was speechless. He had another.

"Meh, they taste unreal! I've never tasted ANYTHING like them in my life!" he declared.

Meh just smiled and said, "Lulu, aren't you going to eat?"

Lulu caught one of the tiny, flapping shrimp on her spoon, closed her eyes, and opened her mouth to swallow. She dared not chew. It wriggled down her throat, and the flavors exploded on her tongue. She laughed.

"It tastes amazing and feels very, very weird!" Lulu said. She put her spoon back in the bowl. Soon she had gobbled the rest of the wriggling, twirling creatures.

Suddenly, the doors flew open. The head waiter came in looking very serious. He said, "The queen would like to congratulate you on your superb goong den. She says it is the finest she has ever tasted."

Then the waiter bowed politely and left. Meh, Ben, and Lulu let out a giant sigh and started to laugh.

The rest of the dinner went smoothly.
For dessert, Meh prepared sticky rice
with mango, crispy pancakes, and huge
platters of fruit. She also made a
special treat for the kitchen staff—
deep-fried bananas!

CHAPTER 8
MISSION RETURN

As soon as the last meal was served, Meh said, "Follow me. I want to show you something special. Next to the Grand Palace is the temple Wat Phra Kaew."

They walked through the garden, soaking up the smells of the flowers and feeling the breeze. During the day, the temple was full of visitors, but now it was empty, except for Meh, Lulu, and Ben.

As they entered the temple, they took off their shoes. Even though it was dark, it was easy to see from the light of the moon. They walked into a beautiful room. High above them sat a small Buddha statue in a glass case.

"This is the Emerald Buddha," said Meh, smiling as she lit some incense and knelt down.

"It's very beautiful," said Ben and Lulu.

For the first time since they had arrived in Bangkok, Ben and Lulu noticed it was quiet. They left Meh with the Buddha and went back outside.

Suddenly, they felt their wristbands vibrate. A message appeared:

Congratulations, SWAT. Mission complete.

Then a red button appeared marked **MISSION RETURN.**

"Time to go, Ben," said Lulu. "What's wrong with you?"

Ben held his stomach. "I ate something at the market, and now I don't feel very well."

"*That's* why it took you so long. What did you eat?" Lulu asked.

"Fried *jakjan*," said Ben, looking greener by the minute.

"What's that?" asked Lulu.

"Fried cicadas," said Ben rubbing his belly. "They didn't taste too bad. Very crunchy, actually. I brought you back one to try." He reached into his pocket and found the fried insect.

"I think I'll save the fried jakjan until next time," laughed Lulu. "I can't try every exotic Thai dish on my first trip! Let's go home. Three. Two. One."

Click.

MISSION RETURN.

GLOSSARY

bamboo steamer—a cooking tool made of bamboo that's used to steam-cook rice

Buddha—the founder of a religion called Buddhism; the name means "the Enlightened One"

coriander—an herb used in cooking

curries—Thai or Indian food in a spicy sauce

gold leaf—shiny, very thin pieces of gold

goong den—(goong den) a spicy Thai soup made with shrimp

jakjan—(jahk-jahn) fried cicadas

klongs—(klohngz) waterways in and around Bangkok

monks—men who serve Buddha and live in a temple

monsoon—a seasonal storm

orchids—types of flowers

rickety—old and unstable

saffron—orangey-yellow

satay sticks—(sah-tay stiks) meat sticks cooked in a peanut sauce

stilts—wooden poles that make a house sit higher off the ground

takraw—(tahk-raw) a Southeast Asian game played with a small, hollow ball

wat—(waht) a Buddhist temple

wok—a special frying pan used for Asian food

of carbonated water (s
plain purified water b
usually costs a baht on

boiled water
bottle
bottled drinking wate

Chinese tea
cold water

IT COULD BE YOU!

Secret World Adventure Team

Come Travel Today!

A complete list of *Read-it!* Chapter Books is
available on our Web site:
www.picturewindowbooks.com